THIS CANDLEWICK BOOK BELONGS TO:

_____

_____

_____

_____

For Rocky Lawson,
the first pirate I ever met

First U.S. paperback edition 1996

The Library of Congress has cataloged the hardcover edition as follows:

McNaughton, Colin.
Captain Abdul's pirate school / written and illustrated
by Colin McNaughton.—1st U.S. ed.
"Published in Great Britain in 1994 by Walker Books Ltd., London"—Tp. verso
Summary: Sent to pirate school against her will, Maisy Pickles organizes a mutiny among the students.
ISBN 1-56402-429-6 (hardcover)
[1. Pirates—Fiction. 2. Schools—Fiction.] I. Title.
PZ7.M4787935Cap   19943
[E]—dc 20   93-21293
ISBN 1-56402-843-7 (paperback)

Reprinted 2002

Printed in Hong Kong

This book was typeset in PirateSchoolbook Roman.
The illustrations were done in watercolor and ink.

Candlewick Press
2067 Massachusetts Avenue
Cambridge, Massachusetts 02140

visit us at www.candlewick.com

CAPTAIN ABDUL'S PIRATE SCHOOL

COLIN McNAUGHTON

CANDLEWICK PRESS

CAMBRIDGE, MASSACHUSETTS

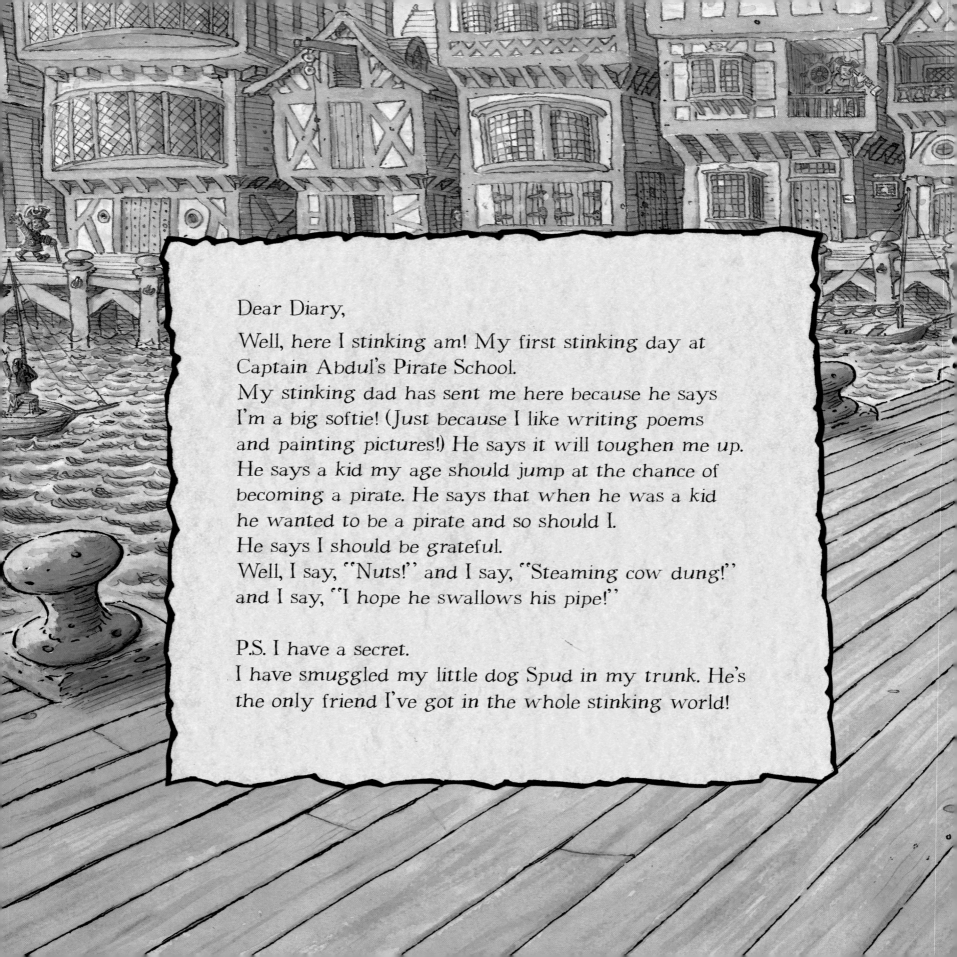

Dear Diary,

Well, here I stinking am! My first stinking day at
Captain Abdul's Pirate School.
My stinking dad has sent me here because he says
I'm a big softie! (Just because I like writing poems
and painting pictures!) He says it will toughen me up.
He says a kid my age should jump at the chance of
becoming a pirate. He says that when he was a kid
he wanted to be a pirate and so should I.
He says I should be grateful.
Well, I say, "Nuts!" and I say, "Steaming cow dung!"
and I say, "I hope he swallows his pipe!"

P.S. I have a secret.
I have smuggled my little dog Spud in my trunk. He's
the only friend I've got in the whole stinking world!

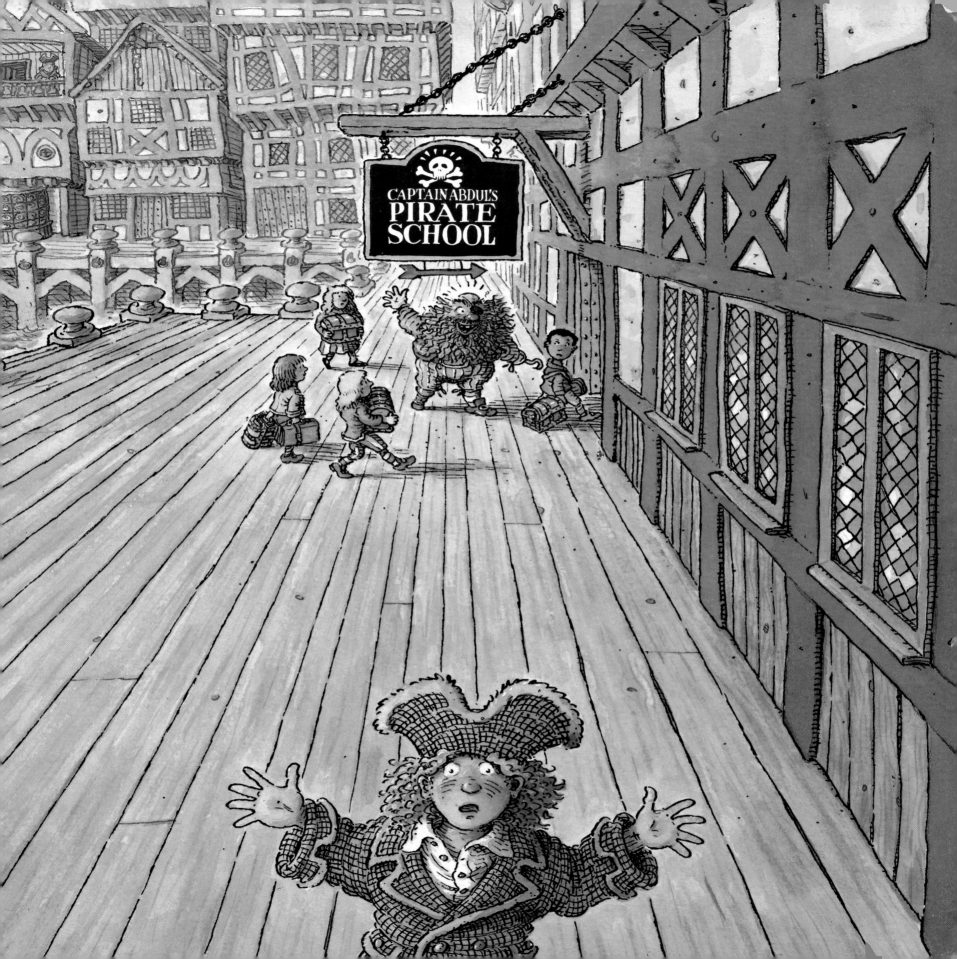

We were met at the door by Captain Abdul himself: hairy, scary, and with more parts missing than a secondhand jigsaw puzzle.
"Follow me upstairs, me little buccaneers," said Captain Abdul, "an' we'll get yer kit stowed away, ooh-arrgh, that we will. Ha-har, ooh-arrgh!"

I was a bit nervous about meeting the other kids but they don't seem too bad—they look just as miserable as me. We then had supper and went to bed, where I wrote this and cried a bit for my mom.

Tom
Tew

Anne
Bonney

Simon
Smee

Jack
Rackam

Ben
Gunn

Frankie
Drake

Samuel
P. Chop

Beryl
Flynn

Mary
Read

Bartholomew
Sharp

O o is for Ooh-arrgh

R r is for Rum

T t is for Treasure

C c is for Cannon

B b is for Bully

S s is for Sword

H h is for Ha-har

X x is for X marks the spot

A a is for Anchor

Dear Diary,

Woke up this morning and stood up in bed. Forgot I was in a hammock—what a headache! I was brushing my teeth when Bully Boy McCoy came in. "What yer doin' that for?" he asked. "If I don't, sir, my teeth will turn black and fall out," I replied. "What's wrong with that?" he said. "Who ever heard of a pirate with nice teeth!" And he confiscated my toothbrush!

Today we studied history. Portobello Billy told us an exciting story about Calico Jack the pirate, set in his favorite place—the West Indies.

Dear Diary,

We were lining up for breakfast this morning when Walker the Plank came over and asked Rosemary Lavender if she was cutting in.

"Yes, sir," admitted Rosemary.

"Well done!" said Walker the Plank and walked away. Today's lessons were math and geography. In math we learned about angles. (You use them when aiming a cannon.) In geography we learned where the West Indies are and how to read treasure maps.

Dear Diary,

The teachers had a party last night! They kept coming up and saying it was much too early to be in bed and why weren't we having a midnight feast or rampaging around the town looking for trouble! "Why, when I was your age," said the captain, "I already had a wooden leg! Ooh-arrgh!" When he finally woke up today he bellowed, "Fresh air is what we need, ooh-arrgh! We're goin' to sea!" For the rest of the day we sailed around the harbor in *The Golden Behind,* learning pirate stuff.

We rolled the teachers out onto the quayside.
"What *now?*" one of the kids shouted.
"We sail for the West Indies!" I cried. "Who's with me?
Who really wants to be a pirate?"
"ME! ME! ME!" they all shouted.
"Good!" said I. "Raid the kitchen, fill the water barrels,
and get the ship ready. We sail *in ten minutes!*"
I wrote a note to our parents telling them what had
happened, *pinned* it to Captain Abdul, and we set sail.

Dear Diary, (six months later)

This is the life! We *now* call ourselves "Pirate pirates" because we only steal from other pirates. On our last raid we found out that pirates from all around the world had heard about our mutiny and, thinking how well taught we must have been, they have sent their kids to Captain Abdul's school! Abdul claims the *mutiny* was all his idea—part of his teaching plan. The scoundrel!

And so everybody is happy: Captain Abdul because his school is a roaring success; our parents because we send lots of treasure home; the kids because they get to sail and swim and fight and fire cannon and rob bullies and stay up all night.

And me? Well, I paint my pictures and write my poems and I'm captain of my own pirate ship! Who could ask for anything more . . .

I'm Captain Maisy Pickles—the happiest girl
in the whole, wide, wonderful world!